The HOUNDS of PENHALLOW HALL

THE SECRETS TREE

HOLLY WEBB

Illustrated by
JASON COCKCROFT

stripes

I

Patch

"There's the bell! Have a really nice half-term, all of you. And enjoy Halloween. Don't forget to do your reading diary and maths worksheets…" Miss Roberts smiled as the whole class groaned.

"It's meant to be a holiday," Lucy grumbled, and Polly nodded.

"I know. It's just wrong, giving us homework over half-term."

"I'll have to take it all to London with me, I suppose." Lucy sighed. "Bet I have to take something out of my bag just to fit it in."

"I'm going to miss you!" Polly said as she stuffed her homework diary into her backpack. "I mean, I'm sure you'll have a great time with your dad, but it'll be weird, not having you around. And you know who else is going to miss you?" she added. "Skip! I hope your gran's bought him some special dog treats."

Lucy laughed. "Yes, she did, and a new rope toy. He'll be OK. Sometimes I think Gran loves him even more than I do. He'll be spoilt by the time I come back." She glanced at her watch. "I'd better go. I have to catch a train from Penbridge with Mum and we haven't got much time to get there."

The two girls grabbed their bags and coats and then hurried out into the playground.

"Oh look!" Polly pointed over to the gate. "Your mum and your gran – and Skip!"

"They brought him!" Lucy said excitedly, starting to run.

"We thought you'd like to walk home with him," Lucy's mum said, giving her a hug as the two girls rushed up.

"He looks so beautiful now, with his proper collar and his fur so clean and brushed," Polly said admiringly. Skip was a stray dog that Polly and Lucy had found in the grounds of Penhallow Hall and he had been adopted as one of the Penhallow dogs, sharing their magical bond.

Now Skip lived with Lucy and he clearly adored her. His tail was wagging so fast that Polly could hardly see it, and he was whining with excitement.

"Sorry, Polly," Lucy's mum said. "We'd better hurry back, we've got to get to the station. Maybe your mum will let you come for tea the week after half-term?"

"Or a sleepover?" Lucy asked pleadingly, looking between her mum and her gran.

"Maybe…" Her gran smiled. "Bye, Polly! I should think you'll have a busy week too, won't you? I saw an article in the local paper about all the nice things happening up at the hall."

"Have a good time with your dad!" Polly called after Lucy as the three of them hurried off down the lane.

"I will! Send me a photo of your Halloween outfit!" Lucy yelled, waving. "See you back at school!"

Polly sighed a little. It would have been fun to have had Lucy around over half-term, but now that her dad lived in London, Lucy spent some of the holidays with him. She was going to be away for the whole week so they couldn't even do anything together for Halloween, which was the Saturday before they went back.

It was going to be a fun week anyway, she told herself. Lucy's gran was right. Her mum was going to be busy at work, organizing all the Halloween events for Penhallow Hall. Polly had promised to help out with the decorations and there was going to be a costume parade on the Saturday. There would be loads to do and Lucy had just reminded her that she hadn't even decided what she was going to wear. She was sure she had a witch's hat and some face paints somewhere under her bed but she quite fancied trying to make something new. Maybe even something to do with the history of Penhallow Hall. Since her adventures with Rex and the other dogs, Polly was starting to feel like an expert on it.

She wandered back along the cliff path from the village to the hall, trying to think of good costumes. She could be the Green Lady, the ghost that two of the Penhallow boys had made up three hundred years before. They had been trying to cover up their adventures with the smugglers bringing illegal cargoes into the cove. Polly felt the hairs rise up on the back of her neck. Even though she and Rex had worked out that the Green Lady wasn't a real ghost, Polly was still scared of her.

Once she was back at the hall, Polly stuck her head round her mum's office door but Nina, who worked with Mum in the office, smiled at her round the phone she was holding. "Down at the stables," she whispered. "She's starting to put up the decorations!"

Polly waved to say thank you, and decided to go and get changed before she went to help. She'd feel properly on holiday once she wasn't wearing her school uniform, she reckoned.

As soon as she'd changed, she hurried down to the terrace to see Rex – she usually did as soon as she came home from school. It was a beautiful afternoon. She could see the sun gradually sinking and through the trees there were tiny scraps of the gleaming sea. Polly ran her hand over Rex's stone nose and saw a faint golden tinge run through the weatherworn surface. It wasn't the greenish gold of the lichen flecked across his muzzle or even the faint October sun on his fur. He was there inside the stone, alive and listening to her.

But not waking up.

"Rex…" she whispered again after a quick glance round to make sure none of the visitors were listening. Penhallow Hall was always busiest in the school holidays, but even today there were people all over the house and gardens. Polly was glad about that, of course, since it was her mum's job to make sure that Penhallow did well and made enough money.

Polly couldn't help wishing that the visitors wouldn't all end up in the rose garden though. She could see why they wanted to admire the seed heads in the borders, and the autumn colours on the trees in the little wood that half hid the cliff path and the view down to the sea – the garden was beautiful. But the visitors made it very difficult to have a conversation with a statue without everyone noticing.

"Wake up!" she hissed. But Rex's statue stayed stubbornly grey and solid. The stone figure on the other side of the steps shifted a little and one heavy grey eyelid opened. Magnus's eye glinted darkly at Polly.

"It's too cold," the huge hound murmured in a low growl. He wasn't angry – it was his everyday voice – he was a growly sort of dog.

"It isn't *that* cold," Polly whispered, surprised. She'd actually been quite enjoying the clear, fresh feeling of the air. It went well with the rusty-golden leaves and the faint smell of bonfires from behind the gardeners' sheds. But there had been a frost that morning – it had still been sparkling on the grass when she walked across the lawns on her way to school.

"It's cold and it's damp. Damp gets into our bones, Polly. Leave us to sleep."

Polly sighed and ran one hand down Rex's stone nose again. "Sleep well," she whispered.

"I'll come back later." She walked away across the lawn, looking back every so often at the two statues. Rex was usually so keen to wake up, to gallop over the lawns and race Polly along the beach. They just had to watch out for visitors while he was changing. Only Polly could see Rex once he was awake, most of the time, but in the moment where the statue disappeared and the stone dog sat up, stretched and shook his ears, he was visible.

"I suppose he is hundreds of years old," Polly muttered to herself as she headed round the back of the house to the old stable yard to find her mum.

She wasn't actually sure how old Rex was. He had been part of Penhallow since long before the great house was built, she knew that. He was even older than the great wooden staircase, which was the only part of the medieval hall

that had been kept when the Tudor Penhallows
had built themselves a grand new house. Since
then every generation of the family seemed to
have added something on – but Polly loved the
higgledy-piggledy pile of turrets and towers.

Perhaps statues really did feel the cold more and centuries-old ghost dogs only woke up in warm weather. Polly grinned to herself at the thought, then her smile faded. She had Lucy, of course, but Rex was definitely still her best friend. She didn't want to be without him until the spring.

"Polly! Hello, love! How was school?" Polly's mum waved at her from across the yard and reached out one arm to hug her, and then had to stop and snatch at the massive pumpkin she was carrying. It had started to slip now she was trying to carry it under her other arm.

Polly made a grab for the pumpkin too. "Watch it! School was good. But I'm glad we've got a week off and I've come to help. This is a massive pumpkin, Mum."

"I know, isn't it? And there are quite a few
more. Stephen's been growing them in his
garden. I wasn't sure he was actually going to
let me have them – they're his babies. There's
one he's going to need a wheelbarrow to
move, it's so big! It really would come up to
your waist, Polly – you should go and see. It
looks like something out of *Cinderella*. They'll
be fantastic for decorating the house for
Halloween."

Stephen was the head gardener and he lived in a little cottage that was made out of part of the old stables. The horses had lived in brick-built stalls around the stable yard, with a long hayloft and sleeping areas for the stable boys up above. Polly had always thought it was quite funny that the horses had such a grand place to live. The stables had little turrets here and there, just like the hall, and there was a tiny clocktower above the tack room. The tack room was the ticket office now, while the stalls had been turned into a gift shop, and rooms for craft events and school groups. Even the tattier bits were used to store chairs and tables for when there was a wedding.

"We need to make the stables look really nice," Polly's mum said, a little worriedly. "Halloween's always been a big event at Penhallow and there'll be lots of people coming. I've been trying to think of something new to make this year extra-special but I just can't." She sighed.

"I'll keep thinking," Polly promised her. "Um, what do you want me to do?"

Her mum looked around thoughtfully. "Can you hang up those garlands?" She nodded towards a box spilling over with tiny black bats. "There are hooks to hang them just above the doors, can you see? You'll be able to reach if you stand on that little stepladder. I've got to take this pumpkin over to the tearoom."

Polly hauled the stepladder over towards the wall and peered up, looking for the hooks. She wrinkled her nose – it was all a bit dusty and cobwebbed but she'd promised to help. She could tell that her mum really wanted all the special Halloween events to be perfect. Carefully, she climbed up the ladder and started to loop the string of bats along the hooks. It was easy enough to do but it took some time because she had to keep climbing down the stepladder, moving it along and then climbing back up.

It was while Polly was looking for the hook just next to the old tack-room door that she fell off. She realized afterwards that she mustn't have positioned the ladder correctly, but at the time it just seemed as if it suddenly went sideways. She squeaked and made a grab for something – anything to hold on to. As the ladder toppled over, she managed to catch at a handle on the old wooden door, and ended up panting and leaning against the door, her heart thumping. She'd been lucky not to land on top of the ladder, she reflected as she leaned down to pick it up and noticed she had put the stepladder down on a stone. As it was, all she'd done was wrench her shoulder a bit.

Polly set the ladder straight and sat down on a nearby step, wondering how she'd managed to be so stupid. She rubbed her shoulder and let out a shaky breath. Then she leaned down to stroke the little dog nuzzling at her knees.

Only there was no dog there.

Polly blinked. There *had* been one. A little scruffy terrier sort of dog. Mostly russety-golden, but with black patches and huge eyebrows.

A couple of months before, Polly might have thought she'd hit her head as she fell and was imagining things, but not now. She looked around for the place the dog must have been hidden, feeling excited. There wasn't going to be a statue or painting in the old stable yard, though. She couldn't see anything even slightly dog-shaped. Polly frowned. When she'd woken dogs at Penhallow before, she had always been looking at their hiding places, or even touching them. So what had she done to wake *this* dog?

Polly whirled round and stared at the tack-room door. She had grabbed at a handle as she slipped from the ladder. Or something sticking out of the door, anyway. Now she pressed her hands against the smooth wood, peering at it and searching for some kind of carving of a dog. Then she smiled. The dog was staring at her, almost nose to nose.

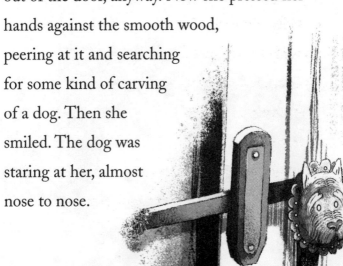

He was on the latch, or rather the bit that stuck out of the door for the latch to drop in. Polly didn't know what it was called. Someone had carved it into a little dog's head, with neat turned-over ears and a wiry, whiskery muzzle. Just like the dog that she'd seen. "So that's where you are," she whispered.

Polly ran one finger over the top of the dog's head, laughing out loud as the wood grew warm, then somehow furry. And then all of a sudden, a little tawny-and-black dog was barking and frisking around her.

She crouched down and fussed over him, but he was too excited to stand still. He raced round and round her, and then went sniffing eagerly up and down the yard. Polly watched him dash about, nose to the ground, wondering what he was looking for. Perhaps he was just enjoying being awake? He must have been shut up inside that door latch for a very long time, even if he had slept through all those years.

She had woken him by herself, Polly thought happily. She hadn't needed Rex to help. Perhaps that meant she was starting to properly belong at Penhallow?

At last the terrier came trotting back to her and sat down at her feet. "No rats," he said, with a huffy sort of sigh. His voice sounded different to any of the dogs she had met at Penhallow before – a soft, countryish burr.

"Oh! Is that what you were looking for?" Polly looked around and gave a little shudder. She'd seen mice sometimes in the parts of the house that the visitors never went to but never any rats. She was glad he hadn't found any.

"Course. It's my job to find them." The dog gazed at her with his head on one side. He had a black patch over one eye, which gave him a daring, piratical look.

"Are you called Patch?" Polly asked. She knew it wasn't a very original name but if she'd had a dog like this, she would definitely have called him Patch, or maybe Pirate.

The dog wagged his tail – a short, stubby tail that wagged into a blur – and barked excitedly again. "Yes! Yes!" Then he stopped and stared at her, and his tail stilled. His ears drooped and he looked worriedly around the yard.

"Who are ye?" he yapped. "I don't know ye!

Where's Jake? Where's my Jake?"

"It's all right!" Polly gasped. "Please don't panic." But Patch was on his feet again, circling and sniffing. "Where is he? Jake? Jake!" He stared at Polly, his upper lip drawn back just a little so that she could see his teeth. Suddenly she could imagine that he would be a demon rat-catcher. "Ye's not Jake," he said again, a low growl in his voice.

"I know, please listen." Polly crouched down, even though she didn't really want to get any closer to those teeth. "You've been asleep for … for a very long time. I'm sorry, but I don't know where Jake is." She didn't want to say that she didn't even know who Jake was. That Jake must have died many years before.

"Where are all the horses? Where are the stable lads?" Patch demanded. "I don't understand! Jake! Jake!"

"There aren't horses here any more," Polly said gently. "I don't think there have been for … for ages. Maybe even a hundred years."

Patch shook his ears, as if he didn't understand what this meant. Then he pressed himself back against the tack-room door, showing his teeth again. He looked terrified.

"I shouldn't have touched the latch again, not without Rex here," Polly muttered. "I didn't mean to scare you, Patch. I just thought … when I woke you up by accident, I thought you'd be happy about it. Look, stay here, *please*. I'll get Rex. He'll explain."

But the little terrier glanced from side to side, growling quietly, and then shot away out of the yard towards the woods. Before she knew it, he'd disappeared among the trees, leaving Polly staring after him and feeling horribly guilty.

2

The Great Tree

Polly raced back through the gardens towards the terrace. She didn't care if there were visitors around – she had to fetch Rex somehow. He had to wake up and help them. What would happen to poor Patch, out in the grounds on his own? It was worse than him not knowing where he was – he didn't know *when* he was.

He probably didn't even recognize half the grounds, Polly thought as she ran. How long was it since he had last been through those woods?

She practically crashed into the stone plinth that supported Rex's statue, grabbing at his paws. Several visitors stared at her in surprise and then looked around smiling, assuming that she was playing a game and someone was chasing her.

"Rex! You have to wake up now!" she hissed into his stone ear. "Please! One of the dogs needs you. I woke him up and I think he's in trouble!"

Rex twitched and shuffled, then glanced sideways at Polly.

"It's all right," she whispered. "No one's looking."

Rex shook himself and sprang down on to the steps, his tail whipping from side to side. "What's the matter? What is it, Polly? You look quite pale." He licked her cheek, gazing down at her anxiously.

"I've lost a dog," Polly panted. "A little black-and-golden terrier. Do you remember a dog called Patch?"

Rex nudged her in the ribs. "Several. Which one?"

"He was a ratter, he said so. And he lived with a boy called Jake. I don't know when, though."

Rex looked thoughtful. "I don't remember any of the children of the house being called Jake. But if this Patch was a rat-catcher, he was probably a stable dog, not a family pet."

"Yes! He was sleeping in the carved latch on the door to the tack room."

"Then he probably belonged to one of the stable boys, or at least one of the boys would've taken care of him. So where is he then?"

"I don't know!" Polly wailed, forgetting to worry about the visitors. "That's what I'm trying to tell you. Patch kept asking where Jake was and I couldn't tell him. I don't think he knew that he'd been asleep. He just seemed to expect Jake to be there. Then he disappeared off into the woods in a panic."

"You woke him without me?" Rex murmured as they set off back to the stables and the woods behind them.

"I didn't mean to!" Polly hurried to explain how she fell off the ladder. "I was supposed to be helping Mum hang up decorations for Halloween. She probably thinks I got bored and wandered off." Polly sighed. Another thing to worry about.

"Halloween decorations…" Rex's muzzle wrinkled. "Turnip lanterns, you mean?"

"Turnips? No, pumpkins. Lots of them. You'll see. And I was hanging up strings of bats."

"Bats? Whatever for?" Rex muttered. "Oh, never mind now. Tell me later." He circled the stable yard, sniffing busily. "Did he run off this way?" he called, looking towards the patch of woodland that spread out behind the stables.

"Yes. He disappeared into the trees before I could follow him. He was just *gone*. He was so upset, Rex. I didn't know what to do."

"We'll find him." Rex sniffed again and then set off purposefully between the trees. "Yes. This way. Hmpf. Got the scent. He went a distance. Fast too…"

Polly hurried after him, looking around for the little terrier. Even though Patch had been fierce and growled at her, she hadn't been scared of him. She had felt how unhappy and frightened he was. She was starting to wonder if there was more to this than just the shock of waking up. Patch had seemed so worried about Jake. Perhaps the stable boy had been in some sort of trouble?

Rex sped up as they came out on to a patch of grassland, not far from the cliff path Polly walked along to school. The turf was rabbit-nibbled to a fine wiry carpet and a huge tree grew in the middle, its trunk so wide that Polly couldn't have stretched her arms around it. She didn't think she and her mum together could have done, either. It was enormous.

"There," Rex said triumphantly, and Polly looked around for the little tawny-and-black dog. She couldn't see him at all.

"Where?" she whispered, and Rex gave an exasperated little huff.

"I forget you don't have a nose. There, Polly, in the hollow of the tree. Gently, now. Poor beast's scared to death." He padded forward and stood quietly in front of the tree. Now that they were closer, Polly could see that there was a dark gap in the trunk where two of the great iron-hard roots seemed to have split apart. The roots crawled out into the turf like reaching fingers and something about them made her shudder. But nestled in the dark slit of the trunk, suspicious eyes glittered. Rex had found him.

"Hello," Polly whispered. "I'm sorry I frightened you. I brought Rex – he might be able to help. He could tell you … things you need to know."

There was a rustling sound of falling dust and bark bits as the dog shifted inside the tree, turning to gaze warily at Rex.

"Come out," Rex suggested gently.

Patch's whiskery golden muzzle appeared and then darted back.

"We won't hurt you. Tell us why you ran away."

"Dunno. Nothing's right." The muzzle appeared again, slowly. "S'all different."

Polly swallowed a sigh, not wanting to distract Patch now he'd started talking. But the sadness and fear in his voice was awful. It made her want to scratch his ears and nuzzle his neck. And to hug him, but she knew that most dogs didn't really like to be hugged.

"Time has passed," Rex said. "It does that."

The terrier lowered his head. "A great deal of time, then? Years?"

"Many years, I think. What do you remember? Who was here when you were last awake?"

"Jake…" Patch whimpered.

"Yes." Rex leaned in and licked the smaller dog's ear. "But who else?"

"Old Foxy were the head groom. Mr Foxham." Patch looked puzzled. "And there was the master."

"That's it. Who was the master?"

"Ol' Sir Anthony."

"Ah…" Rex glanced at Polly. "Sir Anthony Penhallow. He lived here long ago, Polly. In the time after they brought back the king."

Polly stared at him, unsure what he meant. Bringing back the king sounded ancient – maybe like something from the tales of King Arthur.

"Aye, the new king." Patch climbed further out of the tree. "Sir Anthony was at his court in London sometimes, Jake said. And he brought people back with him to Penhallow, for all his grand parties."

"King Charles II, he means," Rex murmured. "The Merry Monarch. The son of King Charles I, who was executed by Oliver Cromwell. Tell me you know all of this, Polly! What do they teach you at that school of yours?"

"There's an awful *lot* of history," Polly pointed out. "We didn't all live through it."

"Huh. Well, Charles II travelled back from the Netherlands in 1660 to be king again, after Cromwell and the Roundheads had been in charge for years. Oliver Cromwell cancelled Christmas, did you know that, Polly? Closed all the theatres, told everyone to dress very plain. Anyway, Sir Anthony and his friends made the most of the good times coming back."

"Always lots of visitors for those parties,"
Patch agreed, his stub of a tail beating against
the tree roots. "Good eating there was then.
Even the stable boys sometimes got a few
leftovers, and Jake, he always shared with
me. Mutton pasties," he whispered, and
Polly noticed that he was drooling slightly.
"Sherbets... Jake had a mouthful once, said it
was like eating flowers."

"Sherbets? What, like sherbet lemons?"
Polly looked at Patch doubtfully. She couldn't
imagine people in the lacy, feathery clothes that
were worn centuries ago eating sherbet lemons.

The little terrier stared back at her, obviously
confused. "What's a lemon?" he muttered.

Rex sighed. "I think sherbets were a sort of
pudding. A bit like ice cream, if I remember
correctly..." He looked wistful. As a ghost
he didn't really need to eat, which was a pity

because he adored food – the smell and the thought of it, anyway.

"So Patch was here more than three hundred years ago?" Polly whispered to Rex. "Do you remember him?"

"Mmmm," Rex agreed. "In snatches. It was a busy time. Guests and parties and music."

"What has happened to Jake?" Thoughts of food had distracted Patch for a moment but it hadn't lasted for long. He had come right out of the hole in the tree now, creeping over the grass to press himself shivering against Rex. "Where is he?"

"Gone," Rex murmured. "A long time gone, I must tell you. All our masters are buried now. But we stay to guard the house and the children."

"He *was* a child," Patch whimpered. "Only a boy! I didn't guard him proper. I should have kept him safe. He was so frightened."

"Why was he frightened?" Polly asked.

Patch stared at her. "I don't know! I don't remember!" Then he let out a sharp growl and snapped his teeth together as there was a rustle and a thud from the tree behind them. Polly gasped, and both she and the little terrier drew closer to Rex.

"It's just a squirrel," Rex murmured, leaning over to sniff at the hole. "No… Maybe not. Something fell. I wonder what it could be – something hidden there perhaps… Reach in and see, Polly."

Polly stared at him in horror. Put her hand into that dark space, where who knows what might snatch at her?

But Rex was sniffing curiously. "Go on, child. You're the only one of us with fingers. What was it?"

Polly crawled forward, her trainers slipping on the smooth tree roots, and then closed her eyes. She couldn't bear to look. She reached into the hole and felt about, flinching, sure that any moment something was going to fly out at her or a spider would run over her hand. But all that happened was that her fingers closed on a small packet.

She drew it out quickly. "Look!"

Rex and Patch sniffed at it as she held it out to them and even Polly wanted to know what it was, now she was safe from the imaginary spiders. "Shall I open it?" she asked, turning it over in her hands. It seemed to be a sort of pouch made of leather, cracked and brittle with age. It had a flap to seal it, tied together with another strip of leather.

"It's Jake's," Patch murmured, sniffing at the pouch. "I forgot. He used it to send notes to Nat – that was his older brother," he added. "Yes, open it up. Perhaps I'll remember."

"Why couldn't he just talk to his brother?" Polly asked, confused. "I mean, even if he didn't work at the hall, his brother could have come up to visit, couldn't he?" She carefully undid the packet, worried that the leather string would fall away in her fingers. Maybe she ought to keep the pouch and show it to her mum instead of opening it. She didn't think it would be valuable but Mum was always saying that it was the little everyday things that told you most about the past.

"Nat didn't live in the village," Patch said, pressing his nose so close to Polly's fingers that she could hardly open the pouch. "This smells of Jake. Just a little."

"So Jake put messages in here and Nat sent him messages back the same way? Didn't they ever see each other? Jake could have gone home to see his brother. He must have got a day off sometimes." Polly fumbled at the leather flap, trying to open it gently.

"Oh yes, they did see each other. Nat would leave a message saying when to meet him. Jake would whistle their song to tell Nat that there was no one around and it was safe to come out.

Always the same tune – sometimes Jake would sing the words instead of whistling. *The Tragical Ballad of Johnny Marks*, they called it."

Polly stopped with the pouch gaping open and stared at Patch. "Why did it have to be a secret?"

The terrier looked confused again and his stubby tail dropped down. "I don't know. It just was. He only met Jake at night, when it was dark and no one would see them."

Polly exchanged a glance with Rex. She was starting to think that Jake's brother sounded very suspicious.

"What's inside there?" Rex asked, peering at the pouch doubtfully. "Anything? I suppose it might have crumbled away to dust by now."

Polly reached in and drew out two pieces of paper – one rolled up roughly and the other folded into a sort of twist.

Patch poked his nose at the twisted piece. "That's a note from Jake to his brother. Don't know what the other is."

Polly unrolled it, spreading it out carefully on her lap. "It's a notice, I think," she said doubtfully, peering at the odd curly type. "The print's faded and it's funny sort of writing, anyway… Look, there's an 'f' there, and I'm sure it should be an 's'. Um, I think it's offering money for something. For 'information leading to capture'… It's a Wanted poster! For 'dangerous and incorrigible' – what does that mean? – 'incorrigible highway robbers'." She looked at Rex, her mouth dropping open. "Highwaymen!"

3

The Secret Code

P atch didn't look particularly surprised.
Rex and Polly both eyed him curiously.
"Is that what your boy's brother did?" Rex
asked, his voice rather stern. "Rode around
the country, holding up carriages and taking
people's money and jewels?"

Patch yawned, although Polly thought he was
actually nervous and trying to hide it. "Might
have been," he admitted. "But Jake never did
anything like that," he added quickly. "He
worried about his brother all the time."

"This notice says that they're offering a big reward, if someone helps them find the criminals," Polly said, still puzzling out the words. "It sounds like they were really keen to catch the robbers. Do you think Jake was trying to warn his brother?"

"We'll see – what does the note say?" Rex nodded to the other twist of paper.

Polly picked it up but she didn't undo it. "Do you think I should? I mean, it's private. It's still folded shut."

"Polly, it's from three hundred years ago," Rex whispered.

Patch sniffed at the paper. "Open it up," he demanded. "I still can't remember – I want to know!"

"Oh, all right." Polly carefully began to unfold the twist of paper, flinching as the edges flaked away. It was so fragile she was worried it would fall apart before she'd even read it.

"So what does it say?" Rex asked, his tail swishing impatiently against her feet.

Polly looked down at the note and then up at the two dogs. "I haven't a clue."

"Bad writing?" Rex peered at the piece of paper. "It looks quite clear."

"Yes, but it's not words!" Polly scowled. "Look, it's numbers – strings of numbers. Ten, forty-one, two, six. It doesn't mean anything!" Then she groaned. "Of course. They wouldn't risk someone else reading their messages, would they? Not if Nat was actually a highwayman. It's in code."

Patch's tail stopped wagging. "So ye can't tell what happened?"

Polly looked at him apologetically. "Well … not yet. I mean – maybe we could try to solve it?" She stared down at the letters. The problem was, she wasn't really sure where to start. They'd done some codes in maths at school but they were very simple – just things like changing letters to numbers, so that A was one. She was pretty sure that Jake hadn't done that – there would be lots more fives, because E was the most commonly used letter, and the fifth letter of the alphabet.

"I need a bit of paper," she told Rex and Patch. "And even then – it looks hard."

"But ye'll try?" Patch licked her hand, his eyes dark and hopeful. "Ye promise? If I know what the message says, perhaps I'll remember." He shivered. "I hate not knowing why Jake was so scared."

They finished hanging up the bat garland on the way back to the house, with Rex and Patch leaning their weight on the bottom of the ladder to make sure she didn't tip over again. Then the two dogs followed Polly up to the flat in the tower, since it was damp and chilly outside, and getting dark. Polly reckoned they could work on the code in her room – Mum wouldn't hear her whispering to the dogs in there.

Mum met her at the door, looking a bit guilty. "Polly! How did you get on with that garland? I'm sorry I didn't come back and help. Stephen had to talk to me about a problem ordering all the spring bulbs he wants."

"It's fine – it looks really good, actually," Polly said quickly as the two dogs slipped past her into the flat. "Um, when will it be dinner time?"

"French bread pizza's in the oven, I was about to come and look for you."

"If I sat under your chair," Rex whispered, "could I have just a very little bit?"

"I'll drop the mushrooms," Polly muttered back as her mum went into the kitchen. "Mum always forgets I don't like them. You still can't really eat them, though, and I guess Patch can't either."

"We can pretend."

Polly's mum had to go back downstairs to the office after dinner. She said she was sorry, especially as it was the first night of the school holidays, but Polly promised her she didn't mind – and she really didn't. If Mum was around, she might want to snuggle up on the sofa together and watch TV, and Polly was itching to look at the code. All through dinner she'd been trying to remember everything she'd ever been taught about codebreaking – but there wasn't much.

Now there were pieces of scribbled-on paper lying all over the living-room table and several crumpled ones on the floor. The string of numbers didn't translate to words at all. She'd even tried mixing two codes together, taking the line of letters she'd translated, and skipping them about, so she'd written B instead of A, and C instead of B. It was still gobbledygook and her eyes were starting to hurt. "Nothing works!" Polly sighed.

Rex was stretched the full length of the sofa, half asleep, and Patch was sniffing his way round the room investigating everything. He explained to Polly that it was all right, there weren't any rats in the flat, it was just that he felt out of practice after so many years and he was catching up.

Polly leaned down to scratch his ears as he pottered past. "I don't know any other sort of code," she said sadly. Then she pushed her chair back, scraping it across the floorboards. "I bet William does, though! He's really into that sort of thing. He told me they used to tap messages to each other in Morse code across the classroom at his school."

Rex peered over the arm of the sofa. "Good idea. Shall we go to the nursery?"

"William is a ghost," Polly explained to Patch as they headed down the stairs from the turret flat again, hoping that he wouldn't be frightened by this. She wasn't sure that he understood he was mostly a ghost too. "He grew up in the house about a hundred years ago."

Patch stopped sniffing the steps and looked at her worriedly. "He's a swell, then?"

"He means a gentleman born," Rex said, seeing Polly's frown. "And yes he is, Patch. But it doesn't matter."

"I'm not allowed in the house. Never." Patch's stub of a tail was low and his ears were pressed flat against his skull. "Jake might run a message to the kitchens, maybe, but I never goes in. When you brought us up here, I thought we were only going to your rooms – up in the attics, that's where the maids live. But I can't go see one of the family."

"The house isn't like that now. It doesn't belong to the Penhallow family any more – it's for everyone to visit. I promise William won't mind that you're here."

"Can't say the same for Magnus," Rex muttered. "He's an infernal snob."

Magnus *did* look quite disgusted by the small rat-catcher but he managed to control himself. Polly thought it was because he was so pleased to see William lying on the nursery floor, surrounded by bits of paper and clearly enjoying himself. Magnus would put up with what he would probably call *low company* to keep his boy happy.

"You've already thought of the simplest sort of codes," William said, his voice muffled by the pencil he was chewing. "I thought you might be right, turning it back into letters and then working the Caesar cipher, but it doesn't fit."

"The what?"

"Caesar cipher. Julius Caesar invented it – it's
what you were trying to do with jumping the
letters backwards and forwards along the line."
He pointed to Polly's written-out alphabet.
"It's a transposition cipher, you jump three

letters forward – Caesar invented it so he could send coded letters. Our Latin master showed us one day when he was in a good mood."

"Oh. So if it isn't that, do you know what it *is*?"

"No." William twirled the pencil round his fingers. "Could be a columnar cipher, I suppose. Which is a bit of a beast to solve since we don't know their keyword. But usually it's a series of letters… I don't see why they'd turn it into numbers as well. It being in numbers like this probably means it's a book code and we haven't a hope of solving it unless we find the book. Which isn't likely, since this was written three hundred years ago." William didn't look as though he minded, though. He was still staring vaguely at the code, obviously enjoying himself.

"Pretend you're talking to somebody who's never seen a book code," Polly said, putting her hand over the message. She'd copied it out, so they weren't putting their fingers all over the real one.

William blinked at her. "Really? You've never seen one before?"

"No! This is why I asked you to help!"

William beamed at her. "Right, I forgot. So, a book code's when both people – the person sending the message and the person who has to read it – they both have the same book. And for each word in the message, the person sending it finds the same word in the book. And they put the page number and the line number and the number the word comes in the line. It's very simple. Of course, there are much better sorts of code to use, using just a keyword so you don't need to have a book…"

William's eyes glazed over again and Polly sighed. "Please don't start inventing new codes!

We need you to solve this one! But … I'm not sure it can be a book code."

"Why not? It looks like one – the way the numbers are set out."

"I'm just not sure Jake and Nat would own books. I mean, this is hundreds of years ago and Jake was a stable boy, he can't have had much money. Would he really spend it on a book? People didn't have to go to school then, did they? It's amazing he could even read and write."

"Oh…" William looked down at the paper thoughtfully. "I see what you mean. What about a Bible, though? Didn't most people have one of those, at least?"

Polly looked at Patch, who was looking between them, tracking the conversation anxiously. "Did Jake have a book? A Bible, maybe?"

The terrier pawed at the ground. "Not that I remember," he said slowly.

"Maybe it isn't that then… I'll keep thinking," William promised. "But the thing is, Polly, if it does turn out to be a book code after all – well, it isn't much good without the book."

Polly left the code with William – actually, she wasn't sure if she'd be able to tear it out of his hands – but she wasn't hopeful. She said goodbye to Rex and Patch, and hurried up the stairs to the flat, thinking about highwaymen.

Even the word sounded dangerous – she imagined tall men in masks and flowing black cloaks. They'd have horses too, of course. Fast ones, which would have been trained not to bolt when pistols were fired over their heads at the coachmen… Were there highwaywomen, at all? Polly wondered. She had a feeling there weren't – most of the dramatic jobs in the past seemed to have been only for boys.

But from what she'd heard so far, Jake's brother seemed to have spent a lot of his time sneaking about in the dark. Being a highwayman probably hadn't been nearly as adventurous as it sounded. And it was all very well rearing a horse in front of a coach and shouting, "Stand and deliver!" or "Your money or your life!" but Polly couldn't help thinking of the poor people in the coaches, and how scared they must have been when they were held up.

Was there something about highwaymen in any of the books in the flat? Polly had read the guidebook to Penhallow all the way through now, but she didn't remember it mentioning highway robbery.

"I'll put the kettle on!" she called to her mum, when she heard the door to the flat opening a few minutes after she got back.

"Oooh, perfect." Her mum slumped down on to the sofa, just like Rex had earlier on, and Polly turned back towards the kitchen to hide her smile.

"Did you finish all the stuff you needed to do?" Polly asked, when she returned with a cup of tea.

"Ye-es. I'm still working on all the last bits for the Halloween celebrations. But I'd love to think of some way to make the parade more special. And I can't. We don't want it to be scary, just fun. Thanks for the tea, sweetie." She glanced at the book on the history of Penhallow that was next to her on the sofa. "Were you reading this, Poll? What were you looking for?"

"Oh! Highwaymen. You don't know anything about highwaymen at Penhallow, do you?" Polly asked, sitting down at the other end of the sofa and squeezing herself under her mum's feet. "I was reading a story with a highwayman in it and I just wondered if there was anything about them holding people up near here."

Her mum frowned, a thinking sort of face that reminded Polly of William trying to solve the code. "There were some famous robberies in Cornwall, I know that. There was a woman called Mary Bryant who was transported to Australia for seven years for stealing a bonnet. Being transported was like a sort of even worse prison sentence, the British had a prison colony in Australia then."

"Just for stealing a bonnet?" It sounded very strict.

"She was *supposed* to be hanged," her mum said, sighing. "The law was a lot harsher in those days. And actually, she escaped from Australia. She and her husband and some friends stole a boat and managed to get away. They got caught again because her husband couldn't help boasting about how clever he'd been. But Mary Bryant was from Fowey and that's not very close to here, and I suppose it wasn't quite highway robbery the way you meant either… Oh! I remember! I'm sure there's something about highwaymen in the records of the local Justices. That people on their way to parties and balls at Penhallow were set upon by robbers."

"Wow… So did the police catch them?"

"Well, there weren't any police then. There weren't really any at all until the Bow Street Runners were started and that wasn't until the 1700s. I'm sure the records about Penhallow I'm thinking of were earlier than that."

"But … but if there weren't any police, what did people do? I mean, if someone was robbed? I don't get it."

"I know it seems strange – there were constables but they didn't really chase criminals, they were more there to do the arresting once the criminals were caught. I think people almost acted as their own police – a bit like someone making a citizen's arrest. That's what happened at Penhallow. The owner of the house back then – he was a Justice of the Peace, which meant he'd be the one in charge of sentencing criminals. I seem to remember he was so furious about the robberies that he organized all the servants into a sort of police force and led them to catch the highwaymen himself."

Polly swallowed. "So … which Penhallow was that?"

Her mum frowned, trying hard to remember. "Oh, I get them mixed up. The one before Laurence – I think it could be Anthony."

Polly nodded. That was the name Patch had said.

"If you're really interested, Polly, we can have a quick look in the picture gallery. Although I suppose it's a bit late."

"No, it isn't!" Polly jumped up. "You can take your tea with you, Mum. Please…"

"Well, it is the holidays!" Polly's mum smiled. "I know there's a portrait of him because he's painted with a set of scales, to show that he's a judge. Judges are supposed to weigh the truth when they listen to a case," she added, as she saw that Polly was looking confused again. "They weigh the evidence in their heads to decide if someone's guilty or innocent. His name will be on one of those little labels on the portrait frame. I think there's a painting of one of those grand parties as well, actually."

"You're not too tired?" Polly said, remembering the way her mum had flopped on to the sofa.

"Not if you pull me up. You know I love showing you this kind of stuff. It's been brilliant having you here, where I work. I feel like you know loads more about my job than you ever did when I worked at the museum back in London."

Polly grabbed her mum's hands and hauled her out of the cushions, and they went down the twisting staircase and through the main house to the long, narrow gallery. It wasn't one of the rooms that was open to visitors, and Polly like to read there sometimes. It had very comfy, tattered window-seat cushions. She couldn't remember the particular paintings her mum was talking about but that wasn't so strange – there were hundreds of them, hanging all the way up the walls.

Polly's mum searched along the walls, muttering to herself. "Now, where was he? I know it was this side. Oh, here look, Polly. It *is* Sir Anthony, it says here."

The man in the portrait had long, slightly curling dark hair and a thin moustache. He seemed to be wearing a grand sort of robe and her mum was right – there was a tiny pair of scales dangling from his hand. He looked – Polly bit her lip because she didn't like to think it, but Sir Anthony looked cruel. As though he'd send all criminals he judged to the gallows without a second thought. It was something about his mouth, the way his thin lips were pressed together. Polly shivered.

"And this is the other one that I was talking about." Her mum crouched down to get a better look – the paintings really did go all over the walls and this one was tucked away in a corner at the bottom. "It must have been an amazing party."

"Do you know when it was?" Polly asked, kneeling down in front of the picture. It seemed very dark at first but when she looked closer, she could see that it was an evening party in the gardens. It was obviously Penhallow too – she could see the terrace in the background, and there were the statues of Magnus and Rex, with strings of glowing lanterns hanging on poles above their heads. "Was it for someone's birthday? Or a wedding?"

"I don't know." Her mum shook her head. "Do you think that's him?" She pointed to a figure with the same curly dark hair, dancing on the grass with a woman in a pink silk dress. He was looking out of the painting and he had that same hard expression on his face.

"Yes," Polly whispered. She was starting to feel a little bit more sympathetic to Jake's brother.

"Maybe we should think about moving this painting to be on display somewhere," her mum wondered aloud. "It's so interesting to see a painting of the house from back then."

"I love the lanterns. They make the marble on the terrace glow gold. Hey! Mum!" Polly jumped up. "You know you wanted something special for the Halloween celebrations? You could have a lantern parade!"

Polly's mum stared at her, eyes widening. "With everyone in their costumes... Oh, Polly, what a fab idea! I've seen photos of lantern parades, ones where people made the lanterns themselves out of paper. I wonder if we've got time to organize some lantern-making workshops? There's a whole week to go before Halloween…"

"I could help – I mean, it's half-term so I'm around. Making lanterns sounds fun." *As long as it doesn't stop me finding out what happened to Jake and Patch*, Polly added to herself.

4

The Tragical Ballad

The next morning, Polly was still huddled under her duvet when her mum came in with a plate of toast. "Morning, sweetie!"

"It's too early…" Polly groaned. "It's practically still dark, Mum! And it's the holidays!"

"I know, sorry. I was just so excited about your lantern idea. I sent some emails about it last night and the volunteers who help with the Halloween celebrations think it's a great idea too. So I've been up early, ordering the special paper and the willow sticks we'll have to use to make the lantern frames. They're going to be delivered tomorrow!"

"Wow!" Polly unrolled herself from the duvet. "That's fast."

"Yes, it turns out that Nina's made them before and she's very enthusiastic. She says she wishes she'd thought of it herself. So she's happy to lead the workshop. And I'm going to ring the local paper to get them to put in something about the parade. It's so exciting! Anyway, you don't have to get up right this minute but I brought you breakfast." She put the toast down on Polly's bedside table. "And something to read, look. I found this in the filing cabinet. It's a folder with photographs of some seventeenth-century documents that relate to the house. Somebody must have been planning to use them for a display. I've made photocopies of them for you, Polly. You might find something about highwaymen at Penhallow. See you later!"

Polly reached out a hand to the toast and blinked thoughtfully at the folder, which her mum had balanced in a crease of the duvet. She was suddenly feeling a lot less sleepy. The documents might give her some clue about what had actually happened to Jake. Yawning a little, she wriggled back, pushed up her pillow and started to flip through the pages.

The first few were all copies of account books from the estate and not very interesting – they listed the rent payments for the various farms that belonged to Sir Anthony and noted the wages for the servants. Polly tried to skim through them – after all, Sir Anthony might have paid them extra money to go and fight highwaymen. But there was nothing like that.

She was about to give up when she found

something entirely different. It reminded her a little of the Wanted poster they'd found in Jake's leather pouch – something about the heavy black type. But this was more like a poem or a song, laid out in verses.

"*The Tragical Ballad of Johnny Marks*," she murmured to herself. It sounded so familiar. Then her heart thumped hard. She *did* know it. Patch had told her – it was the song that Jake and his brother would sing or whistle to signal that it was safe to meet.

Polly turned the sheet between her hands, confused. It seemed odd for it to be just one page. She'd thought at first that someone had torn it out of a book but the edges looked quite clean. The person who'd assembled the collection of papers had added a sticky note to the photograph, which her mum had photocopied with it. *Ballad sheet – 1660s? Odd marks on some lines*, it read. But it was hard to see what that meant. Polly peered at the photo, wishing she could see the original paper. It looked like there might be faint lines drawn under some words. It did seem strange.

Polly looked at it for a few moments more, then she yelped and leaped out of bed, the sheets from the folder flying all over the room. She dragged on some clothes without even looking at them properly and raced out of the flat clutching the photocopy. She galloped down the turret steps, then back up the main stairs to get to the nursery corridor.

It was only nine o'clock and the house didn't

open until ten but there were staff around already. She couldn't go flying into the nursery yelling for William like she wanted to. Instead she dithered in the passageway, peering in hopefully. Lizzie, one of the volunteers, was dusting the huge doll's house and Polly couldn't think of an excuse to get in there, let alone to try and call William.

"Did you actually brush your hair this morning?"

Polly slapped her hand across her mouth to muffle her shocked squeak and ducked away from the door. "Don't *do* that to me!" she gasped. She grabbed William by the arm – flinching a little as the ghost-substance of him gave way beneath her fingers – and pulled him up the passageway into the old nursery kitchen, which wasn't open to visitors. Magnus lolloped after them.

"It looks like you just got out of bed," William said, eyeing her hair sideways. "It's everywhere."

"I don't care. And I *did* just get out of bed, anyway. Look!" She held the sheet up in front of his nose and William took it. Magnus looked over his arm to see what it was too.

"A poem?" William frowned at her. "What are you so excited about a poem for?"

"It isn't a poem. It's a song – *The Tragical Ballad of Johnny Marks*. It's their song! Jake and Nat's song. William, I think this is the key to the code! I don't know, could you buy ballad sheets like this? It wouldn't have cost much, would it? So they could have a copy each." She leaned over his shoulder, pointing at the underlined words. "Doesn't that look like somebody trying to work out which words to use? They've underlined '*You*', look."

All the world draw near,
Come closer this to hear,
A tale most ſad and drear
You will attend,
His tale I will make known,
A boy not yet full grown,
His love left all alone
Her heart to mend.

William snatched the paper closer, gazing at it eagerly. "It could be. Here, look." He pulled Polly's copy of the original message out of his pocket and the pair of them leaned on the windowsill in the dusty old room, scribbling and counting.

"It's easier than using a book," William murmured. "They don't have to do page numbers, it's all on one page. The only problem would be if there was a word they needed to use that wasn't in the ballad. Unless they're doing it letter by letter, I suppose."

"What does it *say*?" Polly moaned impatiently. "I can't work out how the numbers fit together. Are they putting line numbers first?"

"Hang on, I'm counting, shh." William muttered to himself, tapping his pencil along the lines and faintly writing in a number at the beginning of each verse. "I think it's like this – there's fifteen verses. Do you see the way the numbers are written in the message? They're mostly in groups of three or four – and the first pair never goes above fifteen."

"Yes! So the second number has to tell us where the word comes in the verse?"

"I think so. Look. The first number is three, then there's a little gap and then twelve."

Both of them turned eagerly to look at the ballad and even Magnus thrust his muzzle between their elbows. Polly was pretty sure he couldn't read – she knew Rex couldn't – but the excitement had caught him too.

"*Where*," she said eagerly. "Here, I'll write it down. What's next?"

"*Are*. Then *you*. *Where are you* – this has got to be right, Polly. It wouldn't make sense otherwise!"

"I know, keep going. The next word's …
Master?"

"*Master … furious.*"

"That's Sir Anthony." Polly looked at William
worriedly. "Oh, I hope he didn't catch Jake's
brother. Have you see his portrait in the
gallery? He's got such a cold, mean sort of
face."

"Shh a minute, I'm counting… *Price … on …
your … heads…* Hang on, *chicken?*"

"No, wrong line," Polly pointed out. "It's
servants."

"Oh yes. *Servants … sent … catch … you.*
I suppose he missed *to* out because he thought
he didn't need it. This must have taken ages to
write. *Guarding … road … tomorrow … night.*"
William sucked in his breath. "If this note was
still in the tree, Polly, do you think that means
the brother never got it?"

"Probably. Unless Nat put it back but I don't
see why he'd do that." Polly swallowed hard.
"What's the last word?"

"*Run.*"

5

Breaking the News

Even though the message had been written more than three hundred years before, the panic and fear in those carefully chosen words set Polly's heart thumping. Solving the code had been so exciting. She'd felt really clever, working out the secret of the ballad sheet like that. But now she just felt sad, and frightened for Jake and Nat. And how was she going to tell Patch what must have happened?

She went out into the gardens, followed by William and Magnus, and laid her hand gently on the stone fur of Rex's neck. "Can you come and talk to Patch with me?" she whispered. "William and I solved the code. I know what the message says."

Rex shook himself awake instantly and peered round at them all with interest. "You have? Excellent."

"Not really." Polly sighed. "Jake's message was a warning to Nat to tell him that Sir Anthony's servants were guarding the road and they'd be caught if they tried to hold up another carriage. But he never got it, you see..."

"So you think perhaps Nat got caught," Rex murmured.

"Yes. Because he never read it, did he? Nat was probably transported. Or maybe he was even hanged." Polly swallowed hard, thinking back to what her mum had said about punishments for robbers back then.

"But what's really bad is – what if Jake got caught too? Maybe that's why Patch can't remember. If it was something really awful that happened to his boy, perhaps he's not remembering on purpose. Do you see what I mean?"

Rex jumped down from his plinth and gazed into Polly's eyes. "But you're not *sure* anything happened to Jake."

Polly shook her head. "We've only got that one message, so I don't know. But I wouldn't be surprised. They might have thought Jake was telling the highwaymen when the richest guests were coming to Penhallow. He'd have inside information, working in the stables, wouldn't he? Surely the stable boys would have to know when people were bringing carriage horses, so they could have stalls ready for them?"

"We'd better go and find Patch." Rex set out across the lawn. "Perhaps this will help him remember what happened."

"Come on, Polly. We have to tell him," said William.

"But what if what happened is awful?" Polly said, hanging back.

Rex sighed. "He still needs to know."

Patch appeared around the tack-room door as Polly and William and the dogs walked into the stable yard. He looked perkier than he had the day before, Polly thought. His stubby tail bounced from side to side as he raced across the yard and he danced around Rex, yapping. Magnus gave him a look that suggested Patch had better not try that on him.

Rex sniffed at the little terrier and licked his ears. "What have you been doing?" he asked.

"There's a stove in there, where Emperor and Lady Lily's boxes were," Patch said happily. "They were Jake's horses, the ones he had to look after. It was very warm. No one noticed me curling up next to it. Or not quite. One lady did go to stroke me but then she stopped and looked at her hand as if she were cakey."

Polly giggled. "That's the ticket office now."

Then she whispered to William, "What does cakey mean?"

"Umm. Half-baked. A bit silly. He talks a bit in dialect, Patch. Old Cornish. I suppose that's how Jake spoke too."

"Patch," Rex said gently. "We need to talk to you." He glanced around at the stable yard, noticing one of the staff smiling and waving at Polly. "Somewhere private."

Patch's ears sagged. "Can ye get up a ladder?" he muttered.

Rex looked surprised. "I expect so, if you can."

"I been up to the old hayloft. That's not changed." A shiver ran over him, like a ripple of fear at the strangeness of this new world. "'Tis a good place, if ye can get up there. I slept in the hayloft with Jake and the other lads, back then."

It actually turned out to be much harder for Rex and Magnus to climb the ladder to the old hayloft than it was for Patch. They seemed to keep getting tangled up in their own long legs, and Polly and Rex had to boost Magnus through the hatch at the top. He was very heavy, for a ghost. Then he sat on the dusty boards shuddering and peering back at the gap.

"I never agreed to this," he kept muttering. "How am I supposed to get *down*?"

Patch thought it was very funny – the wide steps of the ladder were the perfect distance apart for him – he'd run up and down it several times to show them. Then he seemed to remember why he'd brought them to the hayloft and he sat down next to Rex, the worry showing in his hunched back and flattened ears. "What did ye find?" he asked.

"Polly and William worked out what the note said," Rex told him gently. "You remembered that Jake was frightened, didn't you? We think it was because there were men hunting for Nat and the other highwaymen. The note was a warning to his brother – Jake was worried that Sir Anthony and his servants were going to catch him."

"We solved the code," Polly explained. "You know that tune that Jake used to whistle, the one that you said was his favourite, *The Tragical Ballad of Johnny Marks*? He had a ballad sheet of it. And somehow it ended up in the papers that were in the Penhallow records. I don't know how. Maybe Nat left his copy in the robbers' hideout and Sir Anthony kept it? The message in the tree was Jake telling Nat that the robbers were in danger. He was telling Nat he had to get away!"

It was horrible to watch. Patch stared at Rex for a moment, and then Polly and the others could *see* him start to remember. He slumped down flat on the boards, whining miserably. "He said Nat had to run..." he whimpered. "He was all panicked... Oh, Jake..."

He threw his head up and howled, the saddest, eeriest noise Polly had ever heard a dog make. She wanted to stroke Patch, to tell him it was going to be all right – but she couldn't. She didn't know that it would be. "Are you remembering what happened?" she whispered, pressing herself closer against Rex.

"I remembers him writing that letter. He were frantic." Patch looked around at the bare dusty loft and sighed. "It was in here, but it were different then."

Rex nudged him gently. "Tell us. What happened? Tell us all of it."

Patch crept forward, curling himself between Rex's huge paws and began in a growly sort of whisper.

"Ye have to understand. Jake first came to the

hall after his father drowned. His fishing boat was lost. It blew on to the rocks one night, when there was a storm. Worst storm they'd ever seen, the men told Jake."

Polly caught her breath. "Oh no!" But she wasn't that surprised. Fishing must have been such a risky life back then. Even now, those rocks were known to be dangerous. There was a lifeboat station just along the coast, and Stephen had told her and Mum that a boat went aground on them almost every summer and had to be rescued.

"Jake was left all alone. His mother had died when he was just a baby and even though Jake did have an older brother, Nat had argued with their father a few years before and run away. He never came back and all the village thought he was dead. Jake couldn't stay in the cottage, not without paying rent and he couldn't earn enough for that. No one knew what to do with him, except send him to the workhouse. So the vicar asked Sir Anthony to take him on as a stable boy – he told the master that he'd taught Jake his letters hisself and he were a bright lad. He said he'd surely be a steady worker."

Patch was silent for a moment and Polly reached out to stroke him but then drew her hand back. She didn't want to break into his thoughts. It sounded as though Jake's life had changed for ever in one night – a little like hers, when Dad had been knocked off his bike. But at least she'd still had Mum.

"Were you his dog before?" William asked quietly. "I mean, before he came here?"

"No…" Patch lifted his head. He was staring into a patch of air where the sun was shining through a chink in the roof. He seemed to be looking at the dancing specks of dust but Polly was sure he was seeing Jake. "I didn't belong to no one. I was here to keep the rats down. Didn't have no one to call my own, not till Jake came. He didn't like the stables but he liked me." Patch's stubby little tail thumped the boards. "I was his dog then."

Polly blinked and there was another boy sitting with them in the hayloft – except that now the room was stacked with mounds of sweet-smelling hay. The boy was wearing breeches made of some rough fabric and a tattered shirt. He was curled up on one of the piles and Patch was with him, stretched half asleep in his lap.

Polly held still, not wanting to move in case she frightened the vision – ghost, whatever it was – away. But she swivelled her eyes

sideways to look at Rex. Patch was no longer
curled up between the great hound's paws – it
was as though he had transported himself back
into the past and taken them with him.

"They all think he's dead," the boy murmured. "That's what they say in the village. That it was bad luck that I was left all alone and I didn't even have my brother to look after me." He ran his hand over Patch's ears and the little dog squirmed with happiness. "Nat isn't dead, though, ye know. It's a secret."

He chuckled and rubbed Patch's ears again. "Not that ye's going to tell anyone, are ye? He comes to visit me, sometimes." He looked around the hayloft rather miserably. "I wish he'd come and take me away from here. Old Foxy keeps calling me a stupid, gawky lad but I've only been here a week! I don't want to work in a stables, I don't know anything about horses. They wouldn't let me work on the boats, they said I was too young."

He was silent for a moment and then he went on, "Nat *will* come and take me away.

And he'll take ye too, Patch. I wouldn't leave ye behind. He won't mind me having a dog, he never minds anything. He's almost a gentleman now, my brother. He has the grandest clothes, all black. And he brings me comfits, the liquorice ones I like best, and ballad sheets."

He pulled a wodge of folded paper out of the pocket of his breeches and laid it next to Patch's nose. Leaning forward, Polly could see that the papers were ballad sheets – and the one on the top was the same song that she'd seen before, *The Tragical Ballad of Johnny Marks*.

"Nat's got lots of friends, *good* friends. They…" He hesitated, even though he knew he was alone with the dog. "They rob carriages. It isn't wrong, Nat says. What's wrong is the money some of those people have. Gold and jewels and all manner of fine things. Why shouldn't us have some of that too? Dad always worked every hour God sends and he never had clothes like Nat's. It's not fair for those lords and ladies to have all that. It *isn't* wrong to take it," he said again, but there was something in his voice that made Polly think he knew it was. She found it hard to think kindly of Nat, but it was clear that Jake adored him – his wonderful older brother, who turned up every so often out of the blue and brought him presents.

"I don't know how us'll meet up now," Jake muttered, sinking his chin to rest on Patch's head. "I can't go off down to the beach of a night, not without one of the other boys seeing me. What if I don't ever see him again, Patch? He won't know I'm here. He doesn't even know what happened to Dad.

I wish I knew what to do..."

Then it was as if time shifted and the scene reset itself – Polly almost saw it, the lurch between. The hayloft was shadowy now, the golden sunlight gone. Instead there was a colder look to the place and Polly wondered how the stable boys could bear to sleep up there through the winter. She supposed they just didn't have a choice. Jake must have been glad of Patch's warmth, snuggled up against him.

"The others'll be coming up here soon," the boy muttered. He was sitting cross-legged on the floor of the loft, with a stone bottle of ink next to him and he was dipping in a draggled quill. Patch was watching him, looking as though he'd like to nibble on the feather pen. "Haven't got long. I got to warn him, Patch! Sir Anthony, he's some mazed now, since that Lady Alice got her necklace taken by the highwaymen. Storming about he be, the maids told us, all red in the face. He's not going to stand for it, he do want them caught. He'll have them hanged, I know it."

He glanced over at the ballad sheet, propped up against a bale of hay, frowning. *He's counting in his head*, Polly thought.

"He's writing the letter!" William whispered in her ear. "The letter you found!" He sounded fascinated.

"There…" Jake pushed the cork into the bottle of ink, and his eyes widened as a scuffling and a creaking began down below. He hustled away the ink bottle and the quill under an old blanket, and stuffed his letter and the ballad sheet into his pocket.

"Jake! Where art'a? You up there? Old Foxy's after you. Says you need to saddle up Emperor for Master Jeremy."

"I'm coming!"

As they watched, the boy and the dog flickered and faded. It was just Polly and William and Rex and Magnus left behind, staring at the dust motes dancing in the autumn sun.

6

Worried and Waiting

Polly hadn't quite realized what she was getting herself into when she'd suggested a lantern parade. Everyone seemed to be rushing around talking about how to fix the lantern frames together and stick down the special tissue paper for covering them, and whether to use real candles to light them up, or battery ones. (The battery ones, Mum and Nina had decided. Real ones were just too dangerous.) The workshops were popular with the families visiting and lots of them had said that they were going to come back on the

Saturday evening for the parade.

Nina had shown Polly how to make a lantern, which was a bit fiddly but not actually that difficult, and recruited her to help with the workshops. She said it was really useful to have another pair of hands and someone else who knew what they were doing. Mum said she might even be able to pay Polly a bit of extra pocket money to help. This was all great, except it meant there was loads of time when Polly *wasn't* helping Patch.

Solving the code was all very well but she felt as though the only thing she'd done so far was make Patch more miserable. They'd reminded him how scared Jake had been about his brother and then they'd just left him worrying. Polly couldn't see how they were going to find out what had happened next, either.

"If this is what the week before Halloween's

like at Penhallow, I can't imagine the Christmas holidays," Polly muttered to her mum as she dashed into the craft room on Wednesday afternoon, threading her way through a lot of excited, glue-sticky children with another bundle of willow sticks.

Polly's mum rolled her eyes. "I don't even want to think about it. People started sending me emails about Christmas events back in August. We were lucky we managed to sort all this out so last-minute. Thanks for getting those, Polly. I can't believe we'd nearly run out already. I'm going to have to order some more and we're only halfway through the week!"

Polly placed the willow sticks on a table next to the rest of the craft stuff, then sat down with Mum at a table with some of the younger children. "Do you really think everyone who's made a lantern will come back for the parade?"

she asked hopefully as she helped stick on a last bit of paper for a little girl she recognized from the Reception class at school. Billie was supposed to be making a lantern in a triangle shape, but it looked more like a hedgehog.

"I'm coming! Mum said," Billie put in. "I'm going to wear my white mouse costume. Look, it's finished!"

"It looks … excellent." Polly changed the subject quickly. "A white mouse costume sounds good. I don't know what I'm wearing. I'll probably be a witch. Mum, have you got any stripey tights?"

"No… We could maybe get some." Polly's mum brushed her hair out of her eyes with a gluey hand and then flinched as she realized the glue and some bits of paper were now in her fringe. "Oh well. Have you seen what Nina's making over there, Polly?" She pointed over at the central table, where Nina was building a huge framework out of willow sticks and tape. "Come and see."

It was hard to tell what the shape was without the special paper to cover the gaps between the sticks but as Polly came closer, she suddenly saw that it was a dog. A long-legged dog, his paws stretched out to run. "Oh! He's beautiful!" she told Nina.

"He's nice, isn't he?" Nina beamed at her. "The funny thing is, I never thought of making a dog. I was planning on doing a pumpkin, but then it was almost like he appeared. He's going to be massive." She looked worried for a moment.

"I'll help with him," Polly said hopefully. Nina was making Rex, even if she didn't know she was. He was so much part of the house, he just turned up here and there as though he popped into people's heads when they were making things. Polly had noticed that he was actually in a lot of the paintings in the gallery – peering from between the trees, if there was a view of the house, or carved into the stone mantelpieces. Of course Rex would make sure that he was in the parade.

Polly spent the rest of the afternoon helping Nina to cover the dog lantern with paper, then she stopped on her way back to the flat to whisper into Rex's ear how beautiful he was going to look. He didn't move, but Polly was sure that as she walked past him up the steps, his head was held a little higher than usual.

After she had discovered the marked ballad sheet, Polly had packed all the rest of the papers her mum had copied for her back into the folder. But as she was getting ready for bed that night, she noticed a piece of paper half sticking out from behind her bedside table. She really had thrown them everywhere when she worked out that the ballad was the key to the code.

As she picked it up and put it away with the others on the desk where she did her homework, Polly realized that she had never looked at the rest of the papers in the folder. There were definitely a few more that she hadn't seen. She took the folder to bed with her and sat with it propped against her knees, trying to work out which papers she'd already read. Some of the writing was so strange and scratchy that she had had to give up.

Then she came to a page that was definitely new – one that made her heart jump into her mouth. It was headed with the words *An Account of the Trials and Execution and Dying Behaviour of Three Diabolical Robbers.* Under this was a picture, drawn in heavy black lines, of three men standing on a scaffold, obviously about to be hanged. It was a bit like a newspaper article, Polly decided, swallowing hard. She supposed people had bought copies of it, like the ballad sheets. It even had a price printed on the bottom: *One penny*. She really hoped that this hadn't been Jake's copy – since it was probably reporting his brother's death.

Now that she was perhaps about to find out what had happened, Polly didn't want to read it. But she had to – it might tell her what had happened to Nat and Jake. And if it did, she had to tell Patch. She felt so nervous that her fingers had gone cold and it was hard to hold the piece of paper. What if poor Jake had been arrested too?

Odd phrases jumped out at her here and there – "may both old and young take warning by their unhappy fate", "this very morning executed at Penbridge", "brought to a shameful and untimely end". Polly forced herself to skim through the paragraphs, looking for names. She was expecting to see Nat, but the three men were named as John Dyer, Ned Pawley and Jago Pawley. Polly read the names over again, and her breath seemed to come easier. It definitely didn't mention Nat or Jake.

Unless – she supposed Nat might have changed his name when he ran away. Ned wasn't that different a name to Nat, was it? Polly nibbled her nails. And Jago Pawley must be Ned Pawley's brother, surely, and Jago did actually sound quite like Jake. Oh, this was almost worse than not knowing anything. Should she tell Patch? Would it only make him more worried about Jake than he already was? Or perhaps the news would make him remember what had happened. "I just don't know," Polly muttered to herself.

Sighing, she laid the folder on the floor

beside the bed and turned out the light. But as she lay there, struggling to sleep, all she could think of was Patch, whimpering, "Jake… Oh, Jake…"

Polly felt even worse about not having time to help Patch because she kept seeing him when she was down at the craft room in the stables. Patch was always around, dozing by the stove in the old tack room, or busily sniffing after imaginary rats in the yard. Polly stopped to stroke him and whisper hello, when she was sure no one was looking, but she felt bad about it. Patch always looked up at her so hopefully and nuzzled at her fingers, and she knew he was waiting for her to say she'd got more news. She did have news – but she just couldn't bear to tell him.

The horrible description of the hanged robbers was always in the back of her mind. She was almost sure that Ned and Jago weren't Nat and Jake, but only almost. The story had been written to be as sad as possible, with all the details of the robbers praying for forgiveness and worrying about their mothers. If one of them had only been a boy of ten or eleven, Polly thought it would have said so. The writer would have made a big fuss about such a young child being in league with dangerous robbers.

Still, every time she saw Patch's worried, wistful face, she felt guilty. The words seemed to be building up inside her, wanting to spill out. Keeping the secret hurt. She hadn't even told Rex about her latest discovery. She was secretly glad she hadn't had a spare moment to speak to him over the last few days in the run-up to the lantern parade. She was sure he would say they must tell Patch the truth…

Polly wondered what Rex would think when he saw the huge lantern Nina had made. It was finished now, just in time for the parade that night, and Nina had shown Polly what it would look like with little nightlights shining inside. Polly couldn't wait to see the giant dog outside in the dark and all the other lanterns too. She had a star lantern that Mum had helped her to make to go with her witch's costume.

Polly made a face at herself in her bedroom mirror – it wasn't a very exciting costume. She had black school trousers on, a long black top she'd borrowed from Mum and her old witch's hat. She'd been so busy helping out that she hadn't had time to make a really clever costume in the end. She didn't mind, though. It had been so nice, working on the lanterns and spending more time with her mum.

Polly was putting on the witch's hat and adding some green glitter gel to her cheeks to make herself look a bit more magical when Rex put his head round her bedroom door. He looked at the glitter curiously and Polly raised her hands to fend him off. "Don't jump up and lick me! It won't taste nice! Are you coming to the parade? It starts at six, so not for an hour."

"Maybe. But I need you to come with me now." Rex leaned round her to sniff at the glitter pot. "Are you sure it wouldn't taste good? It looks as though it would."

"Where are we going?" Polly asked, frowning. "I can't be late for the parade, Rex. It's Mum's big thing."

"We have to. It's for Patch, Polly. He needs us." The way Rex said it, his voice echoing deeply around the room, Polly knew that he was right. She had to go.

"What is it?" she called as she grabbed her torch and hurried after him down the stairs. "Where are we going?"

"To the tree. The secrets tree, where we found the message."

"Rex, no!" Polly stopped, looking down at him. "It's dark already! I don't want to go out there, not through the woods. It'll be scary."

"You'd be scared, when you're with me?" Rex fixed her with his huge dark eyes, his voice gentle.

"Well … no. I suppose not. But do we have to?" Polly twisted her fingers together. "I don't like that tree – there's something spooky about it. And it's Halloween. I don't *really* believe in all that stuff – witches and vampires and werewolves. But you're a ghost, sort of, aren't you, and William definitely is. I mean, what if something awful happens?"

"It won't. Something important will happen, that's why we're going."

"Is she coming, Rex?" Patch appeared at the bottom of the twisting staircase. "We should go! We're going to find out, I know we are. I can feel it. I'm starting to remember, but I need to go back to the tree. It all happened there, I'm sure of it."

The two dogs ran ahead of Polly as she stepped out into the darkness. It was *very* dark, even though there was a full moon. Thin clouds were racing in front of it, so the moonlight was flickery and strange. And it was cold. At least it wasn't raining to spoil the parade, Polly told herself. She was trying not to be feeble, but the thought of walking through the woods and the clutching, fingerish branches of the ancient tree made her feel shivery. And that was without even worrying about vampires or werewolves. Mind you, she was pretty sure Rex could see off a werewolf – he was very big. She wished he and Patch wouldn't run so far ahead, though…

She was peering through the darkness, flashing the torch about and trying to see where the dogs had gone, when a figure appeared beside her out of the night. He was huge and he was masked, his eyes glittering at her in the dim light of the torch. A cloak swirled around him as he leaned over Polly and she was sure that he was about to grab her. She screamed and whirled round to run back to the house, but the massive figure gasped and stammered, "Polly, stop! It's only me."

Polly turned, looking at him doubtfully. "*Stephen?*"

"Yes, look." He pulled off the mask and there he was, just the gardener in a long dark cloak, looking very apologetic. "Sorry, Polly. I forgot that the mask was a bit scary. It's my costume for the parade."

"What are you?" Polly whispered.

"Oh, I'm a highwayman. Do you like it? A bit different, isn't it? Where are you off to, anyway?"

Polly swallowed. She hated to lie to him but
he was never going to let her wander off into the
woods on her own. For a moment, a little bit of
her wanted to let Stephen take her back to the
house, where it was safe and the highwaymen
were only friends dressed up. But then she saw

the dark shapes of Rex and Patch, staring at her anxiously from the woodland just ahead. "I'm just getting something for Mum," she lied, crossing her fingers and trying to sound calm.

"OK, well don't be long. You don't want to miss the start of the parade. It's going to be a night we won't forget, I'm sure."

Polly nodded. "Yes," she whispered. "I think you're right."

7

The Woods at Night

"It was the same time of year," Patch muttered as he and Polly and Rex crept through the trees. "All Hallows' Eve. I remember…"

"Did you come out to the tree? Is that why we have to?" Polly asked.

"Yes. Jake had a letter for his brother. They used to exchange notes, you see. A few weeks after he'd started working at the hall, he found a letter in one of the horse's stalls. It was Emperor's stall – Jake always did Emperor – there were three stable boys and they shared the work. So Nat had been watching and knew that was probably a good place to leave a note as no one else would pick it up. Jake said it was lucky he'd found it, though, because it was left in Emperor's hay net, and he said Emperor was an old pig and he might well have just eaten it and not cared."

"It was from Nat?" Rex asked, peering down at Patch through the darkness.

"Yes. He wrote that he'd waited for Jake on the beach at full moon, like always, but Jake hadn't come. So he'd gone to the cottage but it was empty. It was only then that he'd found out about their father dying. Nat stopped one of the village boys who wouldn't have known him. He pretended to be an old friend of Jake's father and asked him what had happened. The boy told him Jake was working up at the hall." Patch growled. "And I reckon he went straight back to his cronies and told them they had a man on the inside now. The note told him about the hole in the tree, and said to leave his answer there."

"You think the gang were using Jake to find out when rich travellers would be passing along the road to Penhallow?" Polly asked worriedly.

"They *tried*. Jake said they kept asking but he never knew. And he didn't! He was only a stable boy."

"I suppose that's why they had the code set up," Polly said. "If they thought he was going to be passing secrets."

"He never did," Patch said stubbornly. "*Never*."

"Would he have told them, if he did know?" Rex put in, and Patch was silent. The only sound was the wind rattling the dry leaves on the trees and the scuff of the dogs' claws on the ground.

"I don't know," Patch muttered at last. "Jake loved his brother. He'd have done anything to help Nat."

"So you came out here that night with a letter? That one we found, warning Nat to run?" Rex asked.

"Must have been. Jake didn't talk about it," Patch replied thoughtfully. "He sat there with the sheets of paper, counting the words and whispering to hisself. He were worried, I could see that. He hardly even spoke a word to me that day and he was jumpy as a cat."

"He was right to be worried," Polly whispered. It was too hard to keep the secret any longer. It felt like it was burning inside her. "I should have told you before. I found another paper, not a ballad sheet. It was a notice of a hanging. They did catch them, three of them."

"Polly!" Rex looked up at her, and even in the

faint light from the torch, his eyes gleamed.

Polly turned away. "I'm sorry. I couldn't bear to say. It already feels like we've made things worse."

Rex sighed. "I know – but it's his story, Polly. The truth belongs to Patch, don't you see?"

Polly nodded, feeling her shoulders hunch up. She was ashamed... Rex nudged her gently, his muzzle resting on her shoulder so his damp nose pressed into her neck. "You should have told us," he said gently.

"Tell me now!" Patch yelped.

"It wasn't the right names," Polly said quickly, turning back to look at Patch. "It didn't say Jake or Nat, Patch, I promise it didn't. But … but it did say Ned and Jago Pawley. And I thought that was a bit close. Do you know what Jake's last name was?"

The little dog only stared at her, frightened into silence.

"I shouldn't suppose he does…" Rex muttered. "He'd only have heard him called Jake. Unless the ladies and gentlemen used his surname if they asked him to do something. Pawley – did you ever hear anyone in the stables call Jake that?" he asked Patch gently.

"No…" the terrier whispered. "Only Jake." Then he shook his ears. "I have to know – and now. Us have to get to that tree. I'm starting to remember more of it, the closer I get. Like the path's lighting up in front of my paws."

"So … Jake hid the letter," Polly said. "What happened after that? Do you remember?"

"Yes… Us hid it, just as it was growing dark…" Patch stopped, gazing up at her wide-eyed as he remembered. "But on the way back, us heard him whistling! He was there, in the trees, watching us!"

"Nat was?"

"Yes. And his horse was there with him, tied up to one of the branches. A skinny old chestnut mare. But … but. Ah, that's it. Jake couldn't stop. He'd nipped out to hide the letter when he shouldn't have done and he had to be back before he was missed. He whispered that he'd meet Nat later. He told him to wait at the tree and he'd be back, and it was important – he had news."

"So you went out again that night."

"No." Patch's voice dropped. He sounded almost ashamed as he answered Rex. "He left me behind. He said he couldn't risk me barking, in case I got them caught. I'd never! What was he thinking? But he was determined. He told me to stay and he went off. But I wasn't going to let him! He was scared, I knew that. I followed him. I never thought…"

"What? What happened?" Polly demanded.

"He was angry with me. He marched me back again by the scruff of my neck and he shut me up!" Patch's voice went into a whimper of hurt. "He shut me in that old shed round the back of the stables and he barred the door. I couldn't get out, even though I tried and tried. I wasn't leaving him to go out to the woods alone in the dark. I clawed at the door but it wouldn't budge, and I barked and barked…" Patch was silent, and

Polly shone her torch at him, wondering if he was too upset to talk. But he was staring at Rex, almost as if he'd never seen him before. "It was thee! I barked and I barked and *ye* came," he whispered.

"You did?" Polly squeaked. It was the first time she had heard of Rex playing a part in another dog's story.

Rex inclined his head in a slow nod. "Yes. One of my dogs was desperate and afraid. Of course I came. I always did, even if sometimes all I could do was to be there with them…"

"Ye let me out!" Patch jumped up, dancing excitedly around Rex, leaping up and licking at the bigger dog's muzzle. "It was thee!"

"Yes. Do you want to see what happened then?"

"Yes!" Polly and Patch said together.

"We're almost at the tree." Rex peered forward through the dark shadows of the trees, and Polly shone the torch and saw that he was right.

There was the open grass and the secrets tree, Jake's secrets tree, looming up before them. She walked out into the moonlit clearing with one hand buried in the wiry fur of Rex's neck and Patch pressed trembling against her ankles.

"Huddle down here, at the side of the tree," Rex murmured. "They won't see us. You can watch."

Polly crouched down among the gnarled roots, her hand pressed against the rough bark.

Rex crept underneath her arm. "Lean on me. You don't need to be afraid, Polly, I promise. Turn off the torch." Patch snuggled up close in front of them both and Polly thought that he had far more right to be nervous than she did. She could feel him shaking. It was Patch's own story that Rex was telling and the little dog was terrified.

The night seemed to grow even darker as clouds appeared and covered over the moon, clouds that seemed to boil up from nowhere, and Polly realized that they were back in the past. This was an October night three hundred and fifty years before, and that night there had been cloud.

"Where is the brat?" someone muttered, and Polly's eyes widened. She had assumed from the way Patch had told his story that Nat loved his brother as much as Jake loved him. But this man sounded so angry. Not like a loving brother at all.

"He'll be here, just wait a while." The darkness in front of the tree shifted a little, and Polly realized that there were two men, not just one. Nat had brought another of the gang with him. Or from the way the men were talking, the first man had *made* Nat bring him. He was the ringleader, Polly thought. She could hear the stamping of hooves and a faint jingling. The highwaymen had muffled their horses' bridles with rags so they wouldn't be heard when they stood waiting for their prey.

The moon shone through a break in the cloud for a minute and Polly gasped. There they were, their horses standing quietly by the tree. The fierce-sounding man was huge. He had massive shoulders and the caped greatcoat he was wearing only made him look even bigger.

Beside him, Jake's brother looked thin and young – and scared.

"I promise, Bear. He'll be here. And he'll have news. I told him. I told him we must have news. He's a good boy, he knows what he needs to do."

Polly clenched her fists as she watched Nat stammering and pleading with the bigger man. That was his little brother he was getting into trouble! She had a feeling that Nat was in this way over his head. All his boasting to Jake, and the presents and the good clothes – it was all a show.

At last another figure appeared at the edge of the clearing – a smaller figure, stumbling through the darkness. Polly wanted to shout to Jake to go away, to run, but she knew it would do no good. Even if he could hear her, he was desperate to warn his brother and keep him safe.

"So this is the brat!" Bear lurched forward and grabbed Jake by the shoulder of his worn jacket, and Jake yelped with fear.

"Hey! Have a care of him, Bear!" Nat cried. "He doesn't need you manhandling him. It's me, Jake. I brought Bear with me, he's another of the gang. He's come to hear what you know about the carriages. What you've found out. Ye have, haven't ye? Ye's got the goods? We need it, Jake."

Polly could hear the panic in Nat's voice, but it didn't make her feel sorry for him. She wanted to kick him in the ankles, grab Jake and run. Beside her, Patch was growling under his breath, a nasty low growl that suggested he felt the same way.

"So tell us then, brat. Who's coming? What do the carriages look like? What crests should we be watching for on the doors?" Bear gave the boy a shake, as if he wanted to rattle the information out of him.

"I don't know!" Jake yelped. "I don't know nothing! Leave me be!"

"Whaaaat?" The man's voice deepened and Polly saw where he got his name. It wasn't just the size of him – he growled like a bear too. He gave Jake another shake, harder this time, so hard that Polly was sure she heard the boy's teeth chatter together. Then he roared at Nat, "What's this then? Ye said he'd have the news for us!"

"He does, he will! I promise!" Nat's words tumbled over each other, he was so eager to please the bigger man. "Jake, ye must know, ye *must*. I promised them," he added, hissing desperately in his little brother's ear.

"Don't know nothing," Jake squeaked again. "But ye gotter run, Nat!" His words were muffled though, as Bear shook him again.

Polly whimpered as she looked on, terrified that Bear was really going to hurt Jake. She glanced down at Patch – this must be even harder for him to watch. It was only then that she realized Patch wasn't there. And neither was Rex.

Polly pressed her hand over her mouth to muffle a wail. She didn't want to be out here in the dark on her own. She could be brave – she'd clambered through secret passages looking for smugglers, of course she could be brave. But until now she'd only had to be brave *with Rex*. Never on her own.

She shook herself crossly. Nothing was going to hurt her. This was just like watching a film. (*Except that it really happened!* a voice inside her yelped.)

Where had Patch and Rex gone? Were they taking their old places in the story? Polly leaned forward, her heart thumping faster as Bear's rumbling threats echoed through the clearing. He seemed to be getting angrier and angrier. If Rex had some plan to help, he needed to be quick.

Then she gasped. The moon had broken through the cloud once more, and there they were, watching from behind a tree on the other side of the clearing. Rex's golden-brown muzzle, and Patch's tawny one, much lower down. Watching, waiting for their moment. Polly dug her fingernails into her palms. *How much longer?*

"I've had enough of this," Bear snarled. "The lad doesn't know anything. All this time ye've been promising us heaven and earth, and it was all a hum! Useless, the pair o' ye!" He made a swift movement and Polly saw something flash in the moonlight. She gasped, and leaped up, even though she knew she couldn't change what had happened so many years before. That was a knife in Bear's hand – she could see it despite the dark.

"No point in keeping ye around to blab, if ye's got no use, is there?" Bear raised the knife to Jake's throat, but as the blade gleamed in the moonlight there was a

sudden thunder of barking from the woods
and two shadows broke out of the trees. The
smaller one flung itself furiously at the big
man's legs, ripping and worrying at his long
coat – but the great dark shadow that was
Rex went for the knife.

Polly had never seen Rex like this. Of course she knew that he was a wolfhound, bred to hunt and fight and guard his people. But he was always so gentle when he was with her. He flung himself at the blade, slamming into Bear's arm and knocking the knife to the ground.

Polly sprang up. She didn't care if this was three hundred and fifty years ago, she felt as though she was here and she wasn't going to let Bear get hold of that knife again. Or Nat, for that matter, because she didn't trust him, either. She snatched the knife and darted back behind the tree. She stood there watching with the knife heavy in her hands as Jake rolled away from Bear. Patch herded him back towards the trees with little snarls and yaps, desperate to get his boy to safety.

Bear was on the ground, cursing, as Rex stood over him, growling in his face. Bear knew that

Rex wasn't just any dog, Polly was sure. The man's face was dead pale and he stayed perfectly still. He wasn't trying to push the great creature off. He wasn't trying to get up. He just lay there, staring into Rex's eyes.

At last Rex stepped back and he spoke. Not in the voice he used to speak to Polly, which could be loving or sad or full of laughter. This was a deeper sound, far more eerie – it was a voice that Bear could hear, and Nat and Jake. All of them were staring at this not-just-a-dog.

"Get up, you. Get up and go. Leave my land – and don't ever come back."

8

The Lantern Parade

B ear lumbered up, his breath coming fast, and disappeared away among the trees, his black clothes mingling with the shadows. Polly watched Nat creep away after him, leading the two horses.

Then she looked back as Rex and Patch nudged Jake to his feet and sniffed him over carefully. The stable boy stared at the enormous wolfhound as though he wasn't sure what to believe – had he really heard the dog speak?

"Do ye belong to the master?" Jake asked,

cautiously smoothing a hand over Rex's head. "I never seen ye before. Ye's a grand boy, aren't ye? Did my Patch find ye?" He looked down at Patch and then crouched to make a proper fuss over the little terrier. "Hey! I've just remembered – I shut ye up in the shed. How did ye get out?" He glanced up at Rex and Rex gave him back look for look, his dark eyes serious.

"Surely I should have trusted ye to help. Sorry, Patch. I didn't want ye anywhere near Nat nor any of his mates. I don't like them." He looked around the clearing and sighed. "Nat's gone, hasn't he? I didn't see him go off with Bear but he must have done." He patted Rex again and stood up, saying, "I'd better get back to the stables then, before I'm missed."

He smiled as the two dogs fell in on either side of him and they walked away across the clearing. But as they came to the trees, Rex looked back at Polly and jerked his head, telling her to follow. Polly nodded and then glanced down at the knife – she didn't want it. Just imagining what Bear might have used it for in the past made her feel sick. She scratched a hole at her feet with the tip of the knife and buried it. Then she hurried to catch up with the others.

They headed along the dark path – Polly wanted to turn her torch back on again but she was worried that Jake might see it. She *had* been able to pick up the knife, after all. About halfway back to the stables, Jake suddenly stopped and the two dogs stopped with him, their ears pricking up. Polly nearly walked into Jake and she was almost sure that he saw her. He looked wide-eyed and nervous but he seemed to convince himself that he'd imagined the strange figure walking behind him.

"Dark night, that's all," Jake muttered to himself. "Did ye hear that, Patch? The whistling?"

Polly pressed herself back against a tree out of the way and tried to listen. At first, all she could hear was the wind, Jake's fast breathing and the thump of her own heart – but then there it was. Quiet but definite – a thin, breathy whistle.

"It's Nat!" Jake looked around eagerly for his brother but Polly frowned. She knew that tune too, and she was pretty sure she'd never heard *The Tragical Ballad of Johnny Marks*. It was *Greensleeves*. She knew because she could play it on the recorder from when they'd all had lessons in Year Four. Then again, *Greensleeves* was definitely old – their teacher had told them that a lot of people thought that Henry VIII had written it for one of his wives. Perhaps the ballads all got sung to old tunes, she thought to herself. It would make it easier – the ballad sheet hadn't had any music with it, so people would have to just know the tune.

"Over here," a voice whispered, and Polly shrank closer against the tree as Jake's brother slid past her, holding up a lantern. "Did Bear hurt ye?" he asked anxiously, turning Jake's face from side to side to look for marks. "I'm sorry, Jake. I never thought he'd turn nasty like that."

Polly suppressed a disbelieving sniff. She didn't think Nat should have brought someone like Bear anywhere near his little brother – but then maybe he hadn't had a choice. Once you were part of a gang with someone like Bear, it was probably very hard to get out.

"That dog is staring at me," Nat muttered to Jake, eyeing Rex nervously. "Where'd he spring from, anyway? Does he belong to Sir Anthony?" He hesitated for a moment. "Jake, did ye— Did ye hear him…? Oh … never mind."

"I don't know who he belongs to. He just came to help. Where did ye go, Nat? I thought ye had run off with Bear."

"No…" Nat sighed. "Jake, that's what I came to tell ye. Likes working in the stables, don't ye? More than ye thought ye would when ye started?"

Jake shrugged. "I don't mind it. I've got

Patch, and I like Emperor and Lady Lily fine."

"I can't keep coming back to see ye, Jake. Not for a while, anyway." Nat put a hand on his shoulder. "Bear's gone, that dog of yourn scared him off, but I don't know how long that's going to last. I don't want to keep on this way. It's asking for trouble, Jake. I reckon the authorities are looking out for us."

"They are!" Jake burst out. "That's what I was coming to tell ye, only Bear wouldn't let me talk. Sir Anthony's setting up a trap for ye – the servants armed and ready to fight. He's proper teasy with all of ye holding up his guests. He's jumping, he's vowed he'll have ye all hanged, Nat. Thee has t' go."

"Like a goose walked over my grave." Nat shivered. "I'm going to London. Don't know what sort of work I'll get there, but there's gotter be something I can do. I'll write, Jakey,

I promise ye that." He put an arm round his brother's shoulders and hugged him awkwardly, and Jake huddled against him. He looked really small, Polly thought, smaller than her. He was so young to be left all alone without any family.

She looked on as Nat pressed a coin into his little brother's hand and then hurried away into the wood, leaving Jake staring white-faced after him. Jake watched the trees until the last sound of his brother's footsteps disappeared. Then he crouched down and picked up Patch, holding him tight in his arms, and began to trudge back towards the stables.

"It's better," he mumbled into Patch's ear as they came into the yard. "He's better off in Lunnon. Safer there, without that Bear and the others. He'll write, he said. He will."

Polly could hear it in his voice, the way he

was telling himself a story about Nat making his fortune in London. Telling himself that everything was going to be all right. It made her want to cry.

A gang of excited children rushed past her and Polly pressed herself back against the wall, blinking in the flickering light of their lanterns. There were lights everywhere – strung across the stable yard in great long strings, glowing from deep inside the huge carved pumpkins and shining out from the glowing paper lanterns everyone around her seemed to be carrying. She was back in her own day, she realized. Rex and Jake and Patch were gone, and everyone was shouting and laughing. The parade must be nearly about to start.

But she couldn't bear the brightness and the laughter. Not just yet. Not after being so sad for Jake, left with only Patch as his family.

Keeping to the shadows, out of the way,
she ducked back along the carriage drive and
across the garden to the terrace and sat down
on the steps beside Rex's statue.

Rex was stretched out on his plinth again,
as if he'd never moved. Polly leaned her head
against him.

"You were very brave, jumping for that
knife," she whispered. "I don't think I could do

something like that. I wonder what happened
to Bear. Did he listen to you and go away, or
did he try one last raid? Some of them got
caught, anyway." She shivered, and Rex leaned
down from his stone slab and nuzzled her hair.

"It was a long time ago," he murmured.
"Don't be sad."

"Don't be sad," echoed another little growly
voice, and Polly saw that Patch was sitting

next to her on the step. He licked her hand. "It was ye picked that knife up, so Bear never got it back. Ye did well, Mistress. Ye helped us between ye, and us is proper grateful. Me and my boy."

William and Magnus were standing at the top of the flight of steps too, watching Patch. Magnus was pressed close against William's legs as though he didn't ever want to let him go.

"That parade's starting, Polly." Rex stood up on the plinth, his ears pricking. "I can hear it. Shouldn't you be there?"

"Oh! Yes." Polly jumped up, about to run back to the stables. Then she stopped and took off her witch's hat, tucking it in between the stone pillars that ran down the side of the steps. "I've changed my mind about my costume," she explained to the two dogs. She grabbed one of the long fringey bits she'd cut in the bottom of her witch's cloak, and pulled, tearing it off into a long strip. "Rex, can you bite this? For eyeholes?" she asked hopefully.

"Give it to us," Patch said. "Ye need a terrier for neat work like that, missy. Not a gurt big hound like him."

Polly held the strip in front of him, and Patch ripped it carefully with his teeth, two neat slashes. It left the highway robber's mask a little damp, but Polly didn't mind. She opened up the holes a little with her fingers and tied the strip of fabric around her head. "It's perfect. Thanks, Patch. I'd better go."

The lantern parade was winding up the carriage drive towards the house as she ran to catch it up, peering along the lantern-lit faces to find her mum.

"Polly! I didn't know where you were!" Her mum waved from beside the huge dog lantern. He was strung on four tall poles now, with Nina and Stephen holding them up. As the lantern-dog swayed through the air, he looked like Rex loping along the beach, or galloping along the path through the woods to catch a highwayman.

Stephen grinned at Polly and called, "Like the mask!"

"The dog looks amazing," Polly panted. "Sorry I'm late."

"Isn't he?" Her mum smiled. "This was such a good idea, Polly. We'll have to do it every year."

Polly nodded. *Every year.* That sounded good. As though they'd be here for a long, long time.

A gentle nudge against her hip made her look down and she reached out one hand to stroke Rex. "Do you like it?" she murmured to him. "That's you."

"Could be bigger," Rex muttered but Polly knew he was pleased. He bounded out across the lawns, with Patch jumping and yelping after him in a wild game of catch.

Polly's mum blinked and turned to look out over the grass. "Polly – did you see… No, it must just have been a trick of the light. I suppose the lanterns make a lot of shadows when they're swinging, it's so spooky. Perfect for Halloween."

"What did you see?" Polly asked gently, and her mum laughed.

"Nothing – I was being
silly. It was just for a moment
I thought I saw two dogs
running across the grass.
One huge one and then a
little tiny dog chasing after
him." She put her arm round
Polly's shoulders. "They
looked really happy."

Codes

I loved writing about the code Jake and Nat use to send their messages. Just like William, I think codes are fascinating! Mind you, I know I would be terrible if I ever had to solve one for real... So here are a few famous codes and ciphers (did you know that those are actually different things?) Try sending some secret messages!

Code or Cipher?

Most people don't know this, but codes and ciphers aren't the same. A code is a way of taking a message and making it much shorter and simpler. It works by thinking about what the words or letters mean – so you might send "What time is it?" in code by sending a clock emoji.

The thing to remember is that for a code you need a codebook – like a dictionary that tells you what each codeword or picture means.

A cipher doesn't care what the message means at all! It's working just by symbols. A cipher uses an algorithm, which is like a set of secret instructions that tell you how to change the symbols in your message. It sounds complicated, but it really isn't…

Substitution Ciphers

This kind of cipher works by keeping the letters in your original message (which is called the plaintext) in the same order, but replacing them with the coded message (which is called the ciphertext) by using an algorithm that turns the letters into different ones. Substitution is just another word for swapping one thing with something else.

Caesar Cipher

The most famous substitution cipher is supposed to have been invented by Julius Caesar! The Caesar cipher was used to send messages to his armies. He would write out his message and then change every letter to the letter that came three further on in the alphabet. So A would be D, and B would be E. The algorithm for this cipher is just "Add three".

ABCDEFGHIJKLMNOPQRSTUVWXYZ
DEFGHIJKLMNOPQRSTUVWXYZABC

So Penhallow Hall would be: SHQKDOORZ KDOO! But to make it harder to solve, you can put some extra spaces in to make the words look different: SHQKD OO RZKD OO.

You might think that this was a bit of an easy code for a military leader who was sending out secret orders, but many people in Julius Caesar's time couldn't read at all, so this code would have seemed even more confusing. Enemies intercepting a coded message might have thought it was in a completely different language.

Transposition Ciphers

Transposition ciphers work a bit differently. This time you're keeping the same letters, but moving them around following the secret instructions in your algorithm. Transposition is a word that means moving something from one place to another.

Reverse Order Cipher

One really easy transposition cipher is the reverse order cipher. You write your message backwards. So Penhallow Hall would be: **LLAH WOLLAHNEP**. Or you can work the cipher slightly differently and keep the words in the same order, and just reverse the letters: **WOLLAHNEP LLAH**.

Book Code

Nat and Jake send their secret messages with a book code – even though their book is actually a ballad sheet.

This is a code rather than a cipher, because you're looking for specific words.

This is a really good method, as long as all the words you need are in the book! The important thing to remember is that you must both have exactly the same book. Even if you both have a copy of *Matilda* by Roald Dahl, they may have been printed at different times so all the words will be in different places, and your messages won't make sense.

To send a message, you find the word you want and write down the page it's on, then the number of the line (from the top of the page counting down) and the order the word comes on the line (from left to right).

Can you solve this message? You'll have to guess which book I've used first…

2 7 2 73 19 2 105 7 1
51 14 1 99 16 5 61 8 2

Hold the last page of this book up to a mirror to check your answer!

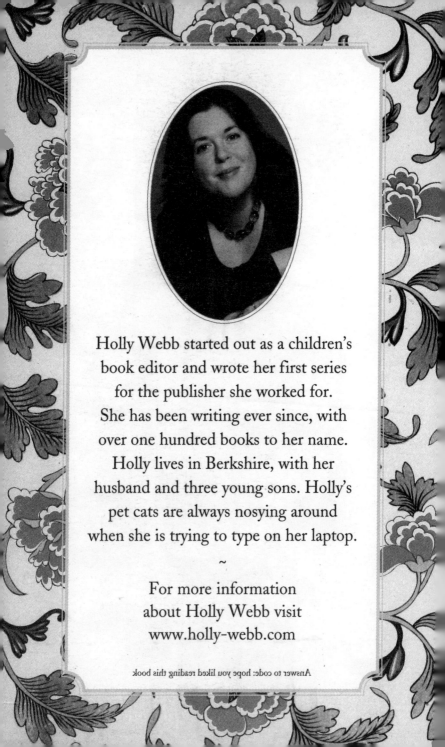

Holly Webb started out as a children's book editor and wrote her first series for the publisher she worked for. She has been writing ever since, with over one hundred books to her name. Holly lives in Berkshire, with her husband and three young sons. Holly's pet cats are always nosying around when she is trying to type on her laptop.

~

For more information about Holly Webb visit www.holly-webb.com